# THE RUMOR OF
# PAVEL AND PAALI

### a Ukrainian folktale

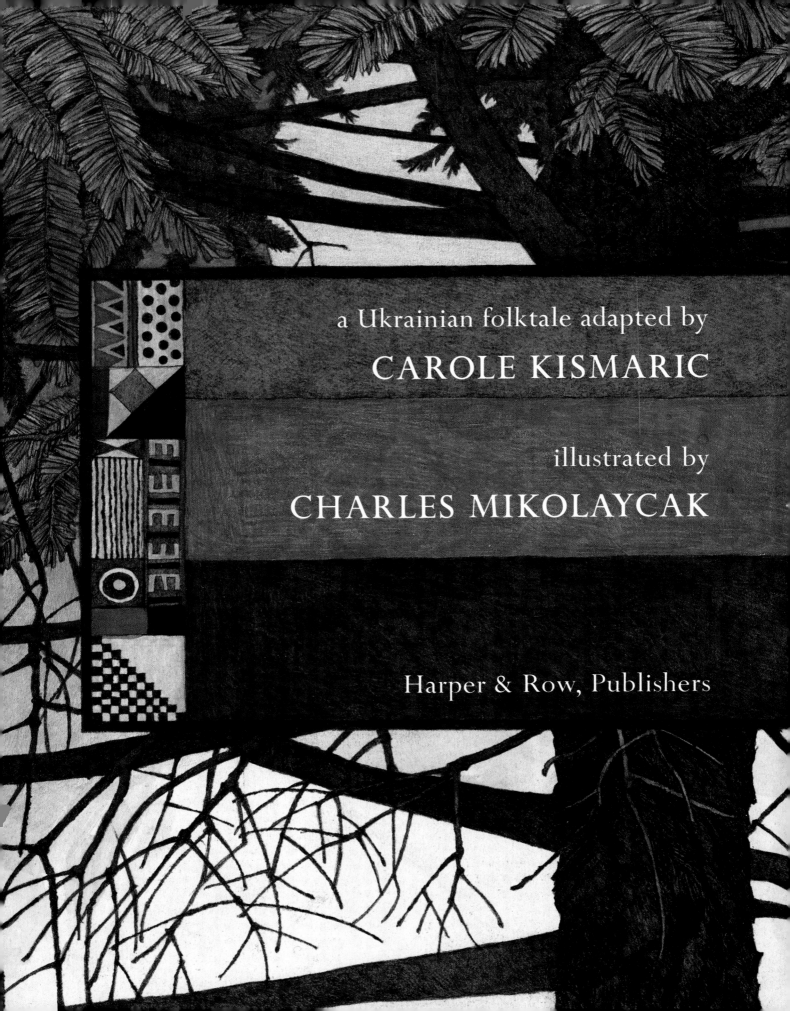

a Ukrainian folktale adapted by

# CAROLE KISMARIC

illustrated by

# CHARLES MIKOLAYCAK

Harper & Row, Publishers

# The Rumor of PAVEL & PAALI

The Rumor of Pavel and Paali

Text copyright © 1988 by Carole Kismaric
Illustrations copyright © 1988 by Charles Mikolaycak
Printed in the U.S.A. All rights reserved.
Typography by Constance Fogler
1 2 3 4 5 6 7 8 9 10
First Edition

Library of Congress Cataloging-in-Publication Data
Kismaric, Carole, 1942–
The rumor of Pavel and Paali.

Summary: When cruel Pavel wins a wager against his
kind twin brother Paali, he exacts a terrible price,
but greed soon leads Pavel to his downfall.
[1. Fairy tales.   2. Folklore—Ukraine]
I. Mikolaycak, Charles, ill.   II. Title.
PZ8.K6198Ru 1988      398.2'1   [E]      87-19958
ISBN 0-06-023277-3   ISBN 0-06-023278-1 (lib. bdg.)

To Ieva, who has always
known the difference.
C.K.

To my twin, John, Jr.
(January–May 1937)
C.M.

I was once told that in a town on a Great Plain there lived twin brothers, Pavel and Paali. Although they once shared a common heartbeat, they grew to be different. Pavel was sour and stingy; Paali was happy and generous. By the time they were young men, Paali understood the world to be a good place and accepted his lot. Pavel always wanted more. As the story goes, one day when the two brothers were talking, Paali, remembering the long winters of the past and how he had suffered, mused, "Though life can be cruel, it is certainly better to do good than evil."

"What an idea!" scoffed Pavel. "There is no such thing as good in this world. It is through cunning and evil that things get done. Good will accomplish nothing."

But Paali was firm. "No, my brother," he said. "I believe it pays to do good."

"Then, since we cannot agree, let us ask the first three authorities we meet what *they* believe. If they answer good, agreeing with you, then I shall give you all I own. If, however, they answer evil, agreeing with me, the little you own will become mine."

"So be it," agreed Paali willingly, and the wager was set.

The brothers walked some distance before they met a
man known to be the hardest worker on the Great Plain.
He was returning from a season of labor.

"Greetings to you," said Paali.

"And greetings to you," said the worker.

"There is something we want to ask you," said Pavel.

"Ask me what you will."

"Which is the better way to live, by doing good or by
doing evil?"

"Oh, dear friends," answered the worker, "I ask *you*.

Where can you find good in today's world? Take my situation, for instance. All summer long I worked hard and made good money in return. Nonetheless, my master's taxes left me with but a meager income. Had I been cunning—lied or cheated him a bit—what is rightfully mine would probably still be mine. No, I'm beginning to believe there is no living to be gained by being honest. I have to answer that it is better to do evil than to do good."

Pavel thanked the worker and turned to Paali. "Well, what did I tell you, brother? I am right, and you are wrong."

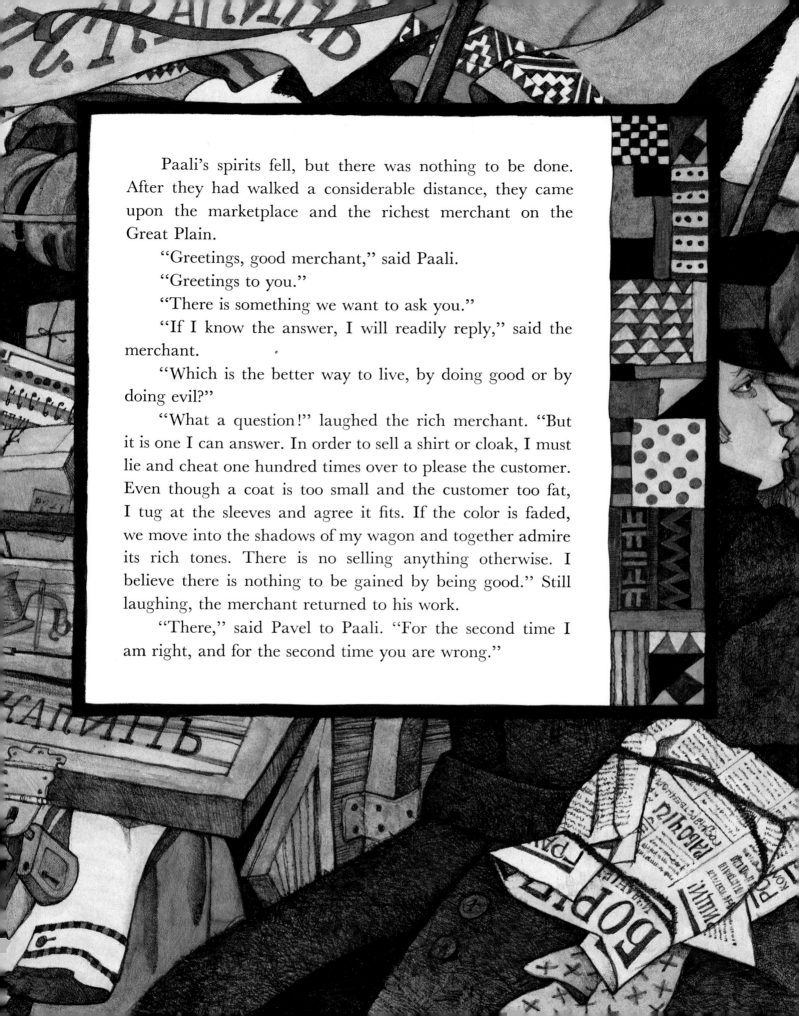

Paali's spirits fell, but there was nothing to be done. After they had walked a considerable distance, they came upon the marketplace and the richest merchant on the Great Plain.

"Greetings, good merchant," said Paali.

"Greetings to you."

"There is something we want to ask you."

"If I know the answer, I will readily reply," said the merchant.

"Which is the better way to live, by doing good or by doing evil?"

"What a question!" laughed the rich merchant. "But it is one I can answer. In order to sell a shirt or cloak, I must lie and cheat one hundred times over to please the customer. Even though a coat is too small and the customer too fat, I tug at the sleeves and agree it fits. If the color is faded, we move into the shadows of my wagon and together admire its rich tones. There is no selling anything otherwise. I believe there is nothing to be gained by being good." Still laughing, the merchant returned to his work.

"There," said Pavel to Paali. "For the second time I am right, and for the second time you are wrong."

Poor Paali was even more disheartened. The brothers continued walking and soon they met a magistrate, a man acclaimed as the most just and wise on the Great Plain.

"Greetings, your honor." Pavel bowed.

"My greetings to you."

"There is something we beg to ask you."

"Ask, my good men."

"Which is the better way to live, by doing good or by doing evil?"

The magistrate thought and thought again before he answered. "My friends," he said, "listen to the words of a

man who has spent his life deliberating between right and wrong. Often, as I lie in bed, unable to sleep at night, I hear again the silvery words of lawyers who have argued a rich man's innocence; I weigh the facts, but I wonder, do I hear the truth? The poor man who cannot afford counsel speaks for himself but, lacking knowledge of the law, often loses his case. It sets me to thinking. As much as it makes me unhappy to admit it, cleverness and cunning impress us in these days, above the plain, honest truth."

"Well, now, Paali, my brother," said Pavel, "I have won our wager. You must give me all that you own."

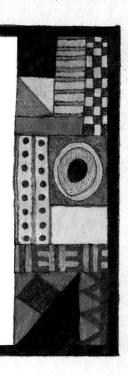

So the deeply sorrowing Paali led his brother to his house. He wept as he watched Pavel seize from him everything he and his wife had scraped and saved for. And so, in a single act, all that had been his no longer was. There was not even a bed to sleep on, a table to sit at, or a morsel to eat. Still worse, Pavel had taken his hoe, his rake, and his seeds. There would be no way for Paali to earn a living. Surely he and his wife would go hungry once more.

For a time Paali and his wife managed to forget their misery, but soon their bellies ached so much that Paali was forced to go to his brother, Pavel, for help.

"Please, brother," he begged, "give me a measure of flour or grain. You left nothing in our house, and we are so hungry."

The cruel Pavel said, "You may have a measure of my grain in exchange for one of your eyes."

Paali thought of his wife, weak with hunger. "So be it," he said. "Take my eye, and may God be with you."

And so, I am told, that is how, for a measure of moldy grain, Paali lost his right eye.

When he returned to his house, Paali's wife stared at her husband in horror. "Oh, Paali, what has befallen you?"

Paali told her, and the two cried and shared their sorrow.

It was after a week, or perhaps two, that the measure of grain was finished. Without telling his wife, Paali again set out for his brother's house.

"Please give me another morsel of food, brother Pavel,"

begged Paali. "What you gave me is gone, and we are once again hungry."

The cruel Pavel answered, "You may indeed have another measure of grain, but in exchange for your other eye."

This time Paali said, "But how can I live without my eyes? Please be merciful!"

"You may have the food in exchange for your other eye. Nothing else will do," insisted Pavel.

And, so they say, that is how, for yet another measure of food, Paali was blinded.

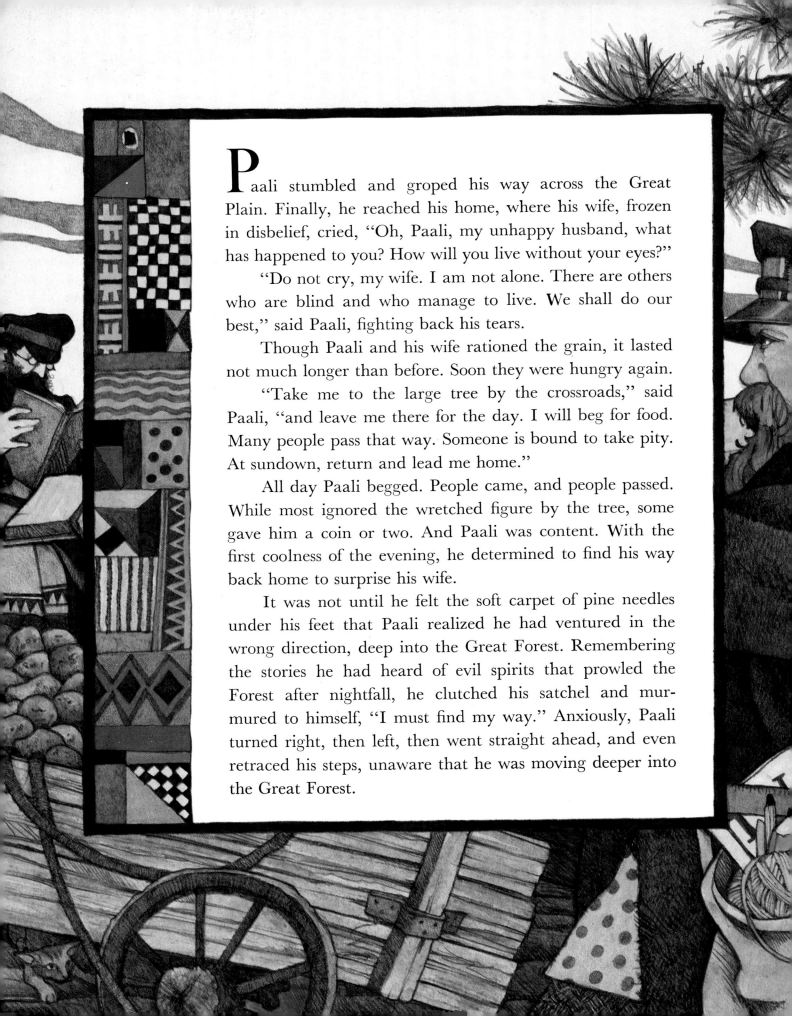

Paali stumbled and groped his way across the Great Plain. Finally, he reached his home, where his wife, frozen in disbelief, cried, "Oh, Paali, my unhappy husband, what has happened to you? How will you live without your eyes?"

"Do not cry, my wife. I am not alone. There are others who are blind and who manage to live. We shall do our best," said Paali, fighting back his tears.

Though Paali and his wife rationed the grain, it lasted not much longer than before. Soon they were hungry again.

"Take me to the large tree by the crossroads," said Paali, "and leave me there for the day. I will beg for food. Many people pass that way. Someone is bound to take pity. At sundown, return and lead me home."

All day Paali begged. People came, and people passed. While most ignored the wretched figure by the tree, some gave him a coin or two. And Paali was content. With the first coolness of the evening, he determined to find his way back home to surprise his wife.

It was not until he felt the soft carpet of pine needles under his feet that Paali realized he had ventured in the wrong direction, deep into the Great Forest. Remembering the stories he had heard of evil spirits that prowled the Forest after nightfall, he clutched his satchel and murmured to himself, "I must find my way." Anxiously, Paali turned right, then left, then went straight ahead, and even retraced his steps, unaware that he was moving deeper into the Great Forest.

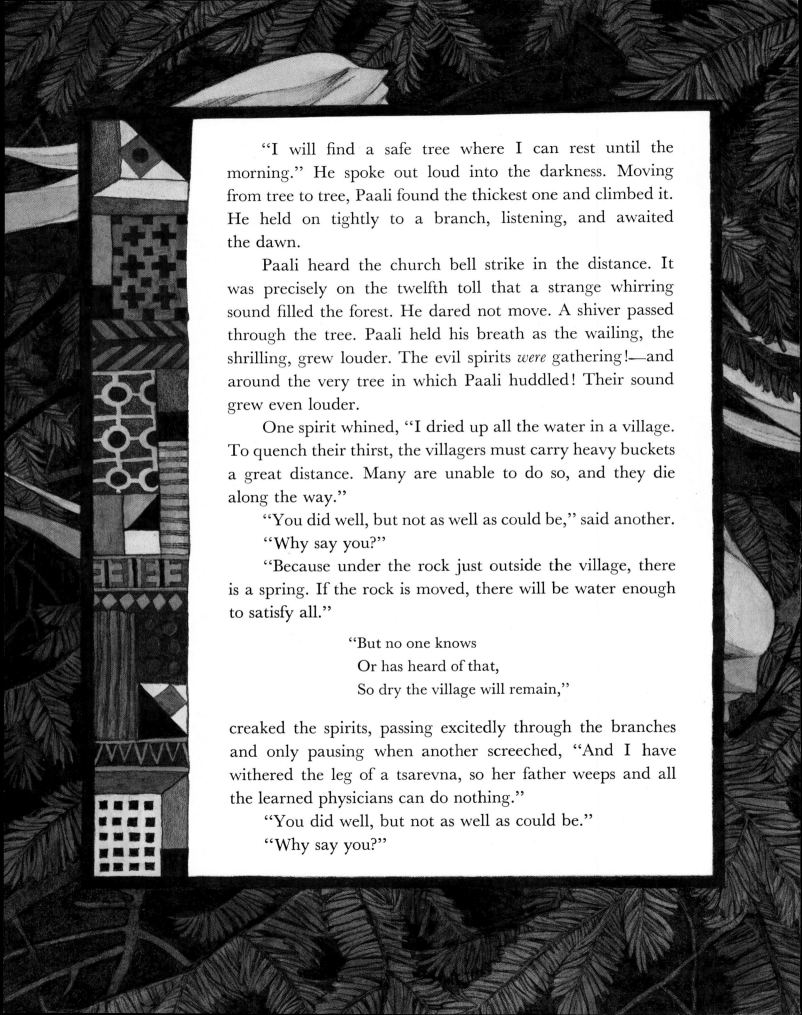

"I will find a safe tree where I can rest until the morning." He spoke out loud into the darkness. Moving from tree to tree, Paali found the thickest one and climbed it. He held on tightly to a branch, listening, and awaited the dawn.

Paali heard the church bell strike in the distance. It was precisely on the twelfth toll that a strange whirring sound filled the forest. He dared not move. A shiver passed through the tree. Paali held his breath as the wailing, the shrilling, grew louder. The evil spirits *were* gathering!—and around the very tree in which Paali huddled! Their sound grew even louder.

One spirit whined, "I dried up all the water in a village. To quench their thirst, the villagers must carry heavy buckets a great distance. Many are unable to do so, and they die along the way."

"You did well, but not as well as could be," said another.

"Why say you?"

"Because under the rock just outside the village, there is a spring. If the rock is moved, there will be water enough to satisfy all."

> "But no one knows
> Or has heard of that,
> So dry the village will remain,"

creaked the spirits, passing excitedly through the branches and only pausing when another screeched, "And I have withered the leg of a tsarevna, so her father weeps and all the learned physicians can do nothing."

"You did well, but not as well as could be."

"Why say you?"

"Because she has only to touch her leg with the rust-red mushroom from under our tree, and she will walk again."

And again the spirits rasped:

> "But no one knows
> Or has heard of that,
> So crippled she will remain,"

and they continued to rush around the tree until another droned, "Better have I done. I made one brother blind his twin for two measures of moldy grain," but a higher voice snapped, "You did well, but not as well as could be."

"Why say you?"

"Because the brother who is blind has only to rub his eyes with the dew that collects under this very tree, and he will see again."

Then, all together, the spirits shrilled:

> "But no one knows
> Or has heard of that,
> So blind he shall remain."

And that is quite simply how the blind Paali heard the spirits' secrets.

As the village cock crowed at dawn, the spirits vanished. Paali lowered himself from his branch. Running his fingers through the pine needles, he collected drops of dew on his fingertips. Wondering, all the time, if the evil spirits had spoken the truth, he touched his eyes—and saw the morning's first light.

"I *can* see," Paali said joyfully. "Now I must help the others," he said, and he searched for the rust-red mushroom.

As he hurried on toward the village, Paali reflected on his good fortune. Arriving, he explained what had to be done. The villagers, scarcely able to believe his words, led him to the rock.

"You must push, and then you must pull, good people,

until the large rock moves ever so slightly. At that exact moment, a great fountain will rush forth." And so it did, running in a wide stream that filled all the wells, the ponds, the brooks, around the village. The people cheered as they bestowed upon Paali what gifts they could gather.